The Timeless Tomorrow

The Timeless Tomorrow

by Manly Wade Wellman

He Who Sees

Blessed or cursed, the moment of sight was coming again.

The light was stealing back into his room curtained so thickly against the coming dawn, stealing back, blue and ghostly from wherever that strange light shone. His twoscore experiences of it were not enough to quiet his trembling. Familiarity with the fringes of that strange land of the soul bred anything but contempt. He could barely hold the two forks of the laurel rod in the tight grip of his hands. His eyes felt wide and strained, as though their lids were bereft of power to open or close.

The mist thinned, so that figures could be seen stirring in it, first dim shadows and then sharp silhouettes. Two horsemen faced each other some yards apart. He caught the gleam of metal. They were armored jousters, on chargers richly mailed and caparisoned.

Beyond them a master-at-arms sat his own mount, with a baton lifted ready to signal, and still beyond him sat spectators in a gallery. It was a tournament of great folk.

The horseman nearest his point of view wore on his surcoat the device of a lion, and his tilting helmet's lowered visor gleamed like fire-new gold. The opponent wore a lion, too, but in a different heraldic pose, and his armor was less ornate. He was of gentrice, perhaps nobility, but not equal in rank with the gold-visored one. That gold visor meant royalty.

Voices made themselves heard, barely, as if from a distance. Ladies were cheering, and the voice of the master-at-arms rang out. He lifted his baton. The two powerful mailed steeds sprang forward at each other, the lances of the opponents dipped their blunt points into position, the armed riders settled their shields into place. Then—

A splitting crash, as of broken timber. The less gaudy rider's tilting lance broke on his adversary's shield and glancing upward, drove its splintered end full into and through the golden visor. A moment later the stricken man spun writhing to the ground. More cries, of dismay.

The victorious rider sprang from his saddle and flung up his own visor. His young face showed dark and concerned as it bent above the fallen one. He loosened the clasps of the gilded helmet and pulled it clear of a bloody, bearded face, more mature than his, with gleaming teeth clenched in pain and the eyes terribly torn away.

The Timeless Tomorrow

Then the mists were gone, and the witness sat alone in the dark, remembering who he was, and where he was, and what he had been doing.

Rising, he dropped upon his brazen tripod stool the robe of strange embroidery with its dampened fringe. Carefully he laid on his desk the forked rod of laurel, and stepped back out of the faint fumes, acrid with strange herbs, that rose from the basin. He went to a window and pulled aside the tapestry that hid it. Dawn was gray out there, and he would be given no more visions tonight. The sun of southern France would be up betimes, warm and cheerful. But he, Michel de Nostradame, physician of Provence, had meditations of the gloomiest.

What had he seen? The face of the young victor in that shadowy tourney-scene was familiar to him—from another vision. Where and when had these things happened—or were they still to happen?

He should burn his books, he told himself. Even if scrying and spying into the future were lawful—and throughout France of this year of 1547 it was a hanging, burning felony—he did not feel that he could endure much more. Better to apply himself to his profession of medicine. Since his visit earlier that year to Lyon, he had come home to little Salon de Craux to find he had lost in popularity, with fewer patients and silver coins than before.

Even a solitary man, with one servant, needs work and money. Michel de Nostradame remembered the days when he was not alone, remembered the wife and children who had died so young in Agen. Too, he remembered his friend, Caesar Scaliger, poet and doctor, who had loved him like a brother and then on a trifling argument grown to hate him like an enemy.

The solitary life here in Salon was a breeder perhaps, of the deep thoughts and the wandering dreams that impelled his spirit across the misty fringe of another time, showing him the wonders and terrors that are not lawful for men to know.

*

Sitting at his desk, he laid out a sheet of white paper, and dipped a quill pen into ink. He began to frame a verse, quickly but thoughtfully, to record his glimpse. That tag of a joust he had seen:

The younger lion shall overcome the old,

In single combat on a field of war.

He will destroy the eyes through a cage of gold—

6

Manly Wade Wellman

Two thrusts will bring a cruel death and dour.

He shook sand upon the little quatrain to dry the ink, and slid it under a sheaf of other verses.

An inner door opened, and his old servant brought him breakfast. He ate a roll of bread and drank from a cup of mingled white wine and water. When he was finished, the servant returned to say that two ladies waited in his front chamber.

Patients, perhaps wealthy. Nostradame hoped so. He washed his hands and glanced at his face in a polished metal mirror. It was a pleasant enough face, with brilliant eyes, a brow wide and high, ruddy cheeks and a firm jaw showing through a fine brown beard.

He walked into the front chamber, a sturdy but not ungraceful figure in his long physician's gown. He bowed to the two ladies who sat there in his best two chairs.

"Messire Nostradamus," the taller and older of the pair greeted him.

Nostradamus—that was his title as a scholar or author, not as a simple man of medicine. He bowed again, studying her quickly. She did not seem in need of healing. Almost as tall as he, with a fine full figure in lordly plum-colored velvet and black hair elaborately dressed and coifed beneath her cap, she looked like a duchess, or perhaps like an ambitious wealthy commoner's wife seeking to be taken for a duchess.

"Madame?" he prompted her.

She smiled in a way she must have known well to be pleasant.

"Messire Nostradamus should know my name without my telling. I know your reputation, fair sir, from my kinsman, the Sire de Lorinville, who entertained you two years back."

"De Lorinville, yes," he remembered. "In Lorraine, he holds the chateau at Faim. I was there at dinner, yes."

"Modest!" she cried, and turned to her companion. "You hear, Anne? Here's a very apostle of humility. He was at dinner with my kinsman, and says so—but nothing of the wonders he did by his magical mind."

So overwhelming was the personality of the taller lady, so insistent her manner, that Nostradame had not found the time to look, even at the smaller. Now he turned his head and met the gaze of her eyes, wide and gray in a thin, earnest face under a dark hood. Her cloak she kept draped effacingly about her, but

The Timeless Tomorrow

Nostradame, the trained anatomist and physician, diagnosed through its folds a slim little body, with such bones as connoisseurs then took to mean good and gentle blood; with not half an ounce of spare flesh, but such flesh as there was was sweet and tender. She was young, and becomingly restrained, but her eyes wanted him for a friend.

"Madame is kind," said Nostradame, "and I would study to deserve such kindness. But her kinsman's tale is no marvel. He but asked what would befall a certain pig in his pens. I said it would make our dinner, and so it fell out."

"Modest!" cried the tall lady again. "Thus was the miracle, Anne, as all Lorraine tells. When de Lorinville heard Messire Nostradamus say that a certain pig would be at the dinner table, he privily bade his cook slay and roast another of the herd—a pig that our soothsayer foretold would be eaten by a wolf. But in the kitchen was a tame wolf cub which gnawed on the pork brought thither, and going for another pig the cook chose the one which Messire Nostradamus had said would be at dinner." She broke off, and smiled on the doctor. "But I am behind-hand in courtesy. I am the Lady Olande de la Fornaye—"

"Enchanted," said Nostradame politely. He had heard of this noblewoman, twice wed and twice widowed, holder of great estates above the town, and storied for her charm and pride.

"And this is my little cousin, the Demoiselle Anne Poins Genelle," said Lady Olande, gesturing with graceful condescension at the maiden in the hood.

"Enchanted," said Nostradame again, musing this time that he could learn to mean it. "Now, which has an ailment and of what sort?"

"I," said Lady Olande, "and my ill is curiosity, of the saddest and sorest. You, sir, shall say my fate for me."

"Your fate?" echoed Nostradame, and fixed her eyes with his. He sat down suddenly. "You ask to know—"

"What will befall me in years to come. My next marriage—"

"My lady," said Nostradame, rapidly and assuredly, "you will not marry again."

"Hélas!" she cried. "Then a sad and pitiful love affair—"

"Nor that. No love affair, sad or glad, is in your future."

"No love affair!" The Lady Olande's voice was strident with protest. "By heaven's gate, am I not made for love, and for love of the best knights in Christendom?"

Manly Wade Wellman

"I tell you your future, as you bid me. You will live without husband or lover."

"Perhaps to travel through France and to other lands—"

"Your travels are over. Madame, your life is not long to run. I foretell as I glimpse it, and not as you must wish."

"Sir, sir, you are a churl and a charlatan." Lady Olande was sweeping to the door. "If you dare expect pay for—"

"Not a stiver for so unwelcome a service," Nostradame said.

"Come, Anne."

They went out together, the little maid glancing back once. Alone, Nostradame smiled to himself, a smile of gentle pity. Perhaps he had done wrong to obey at all that sudden impulse to speak of Lady Olande's fate—it had been no more than a whisper to his inner ear. But he had done so, had angered her. Let her anger be her own reward for insisting.

Others came to his house. An old drover with an infected toe cursed as the doctor's lancet pained him, then called down the blessings of the saints when he was able to set the drained and bandaged foot to earth again. The wife of the town's saddler brought her fevered little boy, and gaped uncomprehendingly as Nostradame advised rest, a liquid diet, and frequent bathing. A blind beggar tapped and whined for alms, and Nostradame gave him a denier and a merry word.

It was almost noon when the door burst suddenly open. Anne Poins Genelle burst rather than stepped in. Her cloak fluttered, her hood had fallen from her disordered brown hair.

"Sir, sir," she gasped, "there is danger—I could not but warn you, for that I saw you at sight to be good and godly—"

"Take breath, child," said he. "There, that is better. Now tell me calmly to whom the danger turns, and in what way I can serve."

She glanced back through the door that swung half open.

"Saints, for your mercy! It is too late, they come! My cousin, the Lady Olande, burns with fury at the prophecy you made her. She has gone to the witch-finder who visits here and named you as sorcerer and ill-doer and agent of the devil—even now they are at your door!"

The Timeless Tomorrow

The Time Stream

Looking past her, Nostradame saw three men striding across the street, the foremost in a black robe like a friar's, the other two with steel-faced jerkins and serviceable swords dangling at their belts.

"Into my study, child," he bade his visitor, pointing to the door. "Thence go into the kitchen and so out the back way to safety. If these are witch-finders indeed, and would accuse me, you must not remain, lest you, too, suffer unjustly."

She hurried where he bade her, and he turned to face the three as they entered.

"And well, masters?" he prompted them genially.

The man in black, for all his clerical-cut robe, had a fierce sharp face and a fiercer, sharper eye.

"To business," he said. "I am Hippolyte Gigny, commissioned by church and king to seek out the rogues and destroyers who, not having the fear of God before their eyes, traffic with the fiend and do sorcery and witchcraft."

"Yours is a good trade," nodded Nostradame. "And how may I, a doctor of medicine, help you to your findings?"

One of the men-at-arms cleared his throat, and Hippolyte Gigny sneered.

"Here's a cool one, and shrewd! How if I say that I know you yourself are a wizard, and as such gallow's-meat in this world and hell's-meat in the next?"

"I would say back that you are sadly wrong," said Nostradame, "and that the layer of the information is sadly a liar."

Gigny's teeth and eyes gleamed mockingly. "You mischief your case when thus you insult the informant—"

"Who is the Lady Olande de la Fornaye," finished Nostradame for him.

"You know, and a demon's voice must have told you, for but now did she accuse you," cried Gigny. "Knave, you are undone. Now shall we search your house. If you prove to have books of black art, charms and instruments—"

He took a step toward the study door, beyond which Nostradame had all three of the articles Gigny had named as damaging. Nostradame shifted position to bar the witch-finder's way, and when Gigny would have persisted, shoved him back so that he staggered and almost fell.

"I am a scholar and a person of gentle blood," said Nostradame. "I will not be treated like a rabbit-poacher or a thief of handkerchiefs. Bring a writ of law before you think to search here."

"My writs of law are of steel," snarled Gigny. "Aho, you two! Draw on this saucy challenger."

The men-at-arms drew, and Nostradame leaped quickly to the wall where hung his own straight sword with its cross hilt and brass mountings.

"Lies the wind at that door?" he said, with sudden gaiety. "Come, then, both of you. I ask only a fair stage and no favor."

His own blade rasped out of its sheath. In a trice he had parried the stroke of the first man to reach him, then a darting threat from his point caused the second to give back. At once the pair saw that they had their hands full—Michel de Nostradame had been a strong swordsman from his student days at Montpellier, and had not let his skill rust for want of exercise.

A little of the stout German cut-and-thrust was in his method, and more than a little of the Italian school, which makes the blade both attack and defense. Two though they were against him, and mailed where he was but gowned, they strove their best and could no more than hold him in check.

But Gigny had rushed past the three battlers, to the door from which Nostradame had thrust him. He tore it open and stepped through. A moment more, and he yelled aloud in coarse laughter, then turned to emerge.

"Cease!" he cried. "A truce, a truce! Put up swords, I pray!"

Obediently his servants gave back, lowering their points, but Nostradame remained on guard. His brilliant eyes were hard and angry.

"God's wounds, I see now this gentleman's wizardry, and would we all could learn from him," sniggered Gigny. "Messire Nostradame—that is your name? You had all good reason to deny us our searching. I have been precipitate here, and a little offending—"

"More than a little," growled Nostradame.

"Then I cry pardon, and do you cry forgiveness." As Nostradamus, too, grounded his sword-point, Gigny came close, nudging the doctor as though to say they shared a pleasant secret. "I am a man of the world, sophisticated—I can see why the charge was placed. One lovely lady ousted from your favor by another—forgive me, I beg again, and also again—send us all such wizard powers, and eke such familiar spirits!"

And he walked out, with a last leer over his shoulder, waving his servants along

The Timeless Tomorrow

with him. Nostradame leaned a trifle on his sword, so that the good steel bent springily, and frowned. Then he turned toward the open study door, to see what matter had so changed the tune of the witch-finder.

*

Of his books, the bronze tripod stool, the water-basin, the forked rod of laurel, his robe with the strange symbols, nothing showed. These had been gathered under his desk, over which had been thrown the cloak of Anne Poins Genelle. And on a couch in a corner she half reclined, the low-cut collar of her gown twitched down so as to reveal a bare shoulder—slim but not bony, Nostradame saw at once. She was the picture, most skilfully posed, of a luresome lady surprised in an intrigue.

"From my heart's depth do I thank you, child," said Nostradame earnestly. "They are gone—"

She rose, twitching her gown into place again.

"It was all I could think to do in that short time. To hide the things they must not find, and to appear to be your reason for secrecy. You are not angry with me?"

"I dread only that you may have brought undeserved shame on yourself. As God is my judge, I am no wizard or devil-companion. But how could you know, and be moved to help my helplessness?"

"That." She pointed to the sword he still gripped. "Its hilt—a cross, and set with a holy name. I read it cut upon the brass as it hung on your wall. And in here—" She pointed again, to the crucifix on the wall, the Madonna on a shelf. "In the presence of the true faith, how could black magic work? Surely, messire, you seek knowledge, but not evil. If you work miracles indeed, right so did the holy saints. I would be your friend."

"You are my friend and my rescuer." He laid the sword on the couch, and stooped to kiss her little hand. In France of 1547 that was a gesture no more than well-bred and admiring, but her fingers stirred in his. The heart of Nostradame, mature and mentalized scholar, was touched. "And how," he continued, "may I serve you in some small way to pay in part my great debt?"

"Be only what you are," she said.

"What do you know of what I am?"

"Perhaps," murmured Anne Poins Genelle, "I, too, have more senses than five. Perhaps I am aware of things beyond this small space and time in which we

12

huddle."

"Child!" In his sudden blaze of feeling, he clutched her forearms. They were small in his grasp, like the forks of the ceremonial laurel rod. "Are you telling me that you, too, know the hour of sight?"

The suddenness of his cry and movement made her shrink in his clutch, and he let go and stepped back.

"Indeed, I cannot say what I meant," she said, recovering. "I only felt what you tried to say to my cousin, Lady Olande, and could understand when she could not or would not. I'll stay a moment, if you talk to me, messire."

He smiled at her. He had not felt so comradely toward anyone in years. Standing over her in his gown of dignity, he was taller than one might think, so broad was his body and so easily did he carry its breadth.

"I think the more, and speak little," he temporized. "Would that speech were as free as thought. Some day it may come to that."

"A prophecy."

"A hope." He led her to the desk, and lifted from it her mantle. There lay his papers. "You deserve my trust, Lady Anne. And, faith, perhaps I need one to listen and believe and understand. Here. Read this first of my quatrains."

He handed the sheet to her. She read aloud, softly:

Seated within my study-room at night

Alone upon a tripod stool of brass,

I saw from out the silent dark a light

That mirrored magic scenes as in a glass . . . .

"That explains how visions come to me," he told her. "Thus I begin my record. How came I thus to study and work? Perhaps by way of my fathers—my grandfather read white magic, and urged me to the like. When I went to Montpellier, to the university founded long ago by fugitive wise Arabs, I learned foreign languages and foreign arts, along with medicine. Books of wisdom did I con in the library—Roger Bacon of England, Albertus Magnus, and certain scrolls by Eastern magi. Yet I did hesitate over their teachings. I think," and he sighed, as if weary a little, "that the hour of sight forced itself upon me."

"It came whether or no?" she suggested; and when he nodded, "When?"

"Within this year. I had returned from my last intention at public honors—I had

The Timeless Tomorrow

been invited to Lyon, as once before to Aix, where I did some service during the plague year. Coming back, I thought to consider worldly wealth and fame a vanity, and to live and study quietly. Then, it began. By chance, or by another will than mine, I did as the verse tells, after the manner of the soothsayers of the ancient Brancchi."

He explained that classical formula of action—the forked rod, the basin redolent of herbs, the moistening of the robe's hem, the tripod stool such as once accommodated the oracle at Delphi.

"By heaven, the ancients knew rare and curious things. Who can say that this wonder is not science? We once would have thought printing sheer magic, and eke gun-powder. Five hundred years gone, my medical studies would have seemed witchcraft. In any case, a vision came, of another time and place. Then others—but read."

*

He handed her another quatrain:
The coffin sinks within the iron tomb
Where dead and still the King's seven children lie,
While ancient ghosts rise from the hellish gloom
And weep to see their withered fruit thus die.
"A dubious mystery," said Anne, giving the paper back.

"Because I dare not set down plain what I see, or how," he replied. "What would be my shrift, if witch-finders like tat vagabond Gigny should read a true account? I made the verse for my vision of an iron-grilled tomb, marked with a lion for coat-of-arms—"

"The lion of the Valois," said Anne at once. "Of our comely king, the Second Henry. I have been to court with my cousin, only three months gone, at his coronation. Henry is a stout rider and weaponer. He tilted bravely against the best of his nobles, wearing the lion upon his surcoat, and on his head a gold-visored helmet—"

"Gold visor!" interrupted Nostradame in his turn. "Heaven's grace, it is what I saw, and indeed only the king may wear such brave armor. Lady Anne, read this. I saw it at the dawn just past."

She read the quatrain he had written that day, and he told her more fully what

14

the mist had drawn away to show him. Anne's slim young face was grave.

"Now, here's a sad wonder," said she when he had done. "It was foretold the king in his childhood that he would die in a duel. His mother scorned the word, for who would dare challenge a royal prince? But if it falls out as you say, in a joust or tourney—when will this happen?"

"I cannot tell. The visions come not in any order of time, though I see and set down things that help me decide. Perhaps the stars in the heavens are shown me, or I hear a word. For this one, I should say the king seemed older than now—a good forty years turned."

"And he is twenty-eight," supplied Anne. "Twelve years hence, or thereon. The year of 1589? And your other vision was of the death of his house of Valois. Will you tell him these sad things?"

"I would need to know him well before making so baleful a prophecy. Remember your cousin's rage at me. I have no fame or position—"

"But you will gain both," Anne told him, with an earnestness so great that it seemed to take her breath.

"You have prophecy for me."

"No, only faith. It is you who see everything and of every time. I am not skilled nor wise in magic. But I feel sure of your future."

"Child, your words make me feel sure, too." He took her hand, in an honest impulse of inspired comradeship. "Happy the man whom you love."

"I love none, messire. My father was gentle, but poor. On his death I came to live with the Lady Olande. Think you she listens to any talk of love save for herself?"

That was enough to sketch for him the life-picture of a poor relation in the home of a woman who ruled her dependents like a tyrant. Pitying Anne, Nostradame spoke of other glimpses he had caught into the future, and of what they seemed to tell of the world to come. Her interest was for France, and he spoke of the rise and fall of powers, of rebellions and defeats and triumphs; in particular of a strange little ruler, a sturdy short man who wore a great three-cornered hat, who for a time would hold all Europe but whose bloody rule would bring the world into arms against him, and finally cause his downfall.

"You speak of other centuries? How clearly do you see distant times?"

"Clearly. Too clearly. Child, it is a horror to see the wars of that far future. Fire

The Timeless Tomorrow

from heaven, wasting away cities, the march of great engines and vehicles, guns as large as giant trees, the advance and retreat of armies as numerous as the generations. Hélas, that man cannot learn!"

"Man shall learn," said Anne, with her air of confidence. "Your prophecies shall teach them."

"How? The future is as rigidly set out as the past."

"Is it so? Perhaps you see but moments, and if men take warning they will be able to change other future moments, for the better."

The two of them could have talked for many hours, but Anne feared what her absence at the house of her cousin might bring. She told him good-day, and again he kissed her hand, which this time did not tremble but squeezed his. And when she was gone, the house and the study seemed to tremble in an afterglow of her presence.

Nostradame grinned ruefully in his beard. Was he falling in love, and with a slender girl, little more than a child? He had thought himself past such things, since the death of his wife. He had mourned her sincerely, that lost wife. She had been kind, loyal and loving, for all she had not once shown interest or even curiosity over his studies of magic and future-reading. Anne Poins Genelle, in two brief hours, had proven herself more understanding and sympathetic.

The afternoon occupied him with another series of patients. He fared out to visit two sick merchants, and found one of them surly, the other depressingly quiet and complaining. He came home to a simple evening meal, and with the fall of night repaired to his study. From the hiding into which the Lady Anne had thrust them he dragged stool, basin, divining rod and robe. Quickly he made preparations for the hour of sight.

He confessed himself weary from the day's adventures. Indeed, he sagged rather than sat on the tripod, but a vision was coming. In his ears rang a faint cry, the cry of a child, and then he saw Anne, as she might be a year or two older, holding in her arms a swaddled infant. She smiled and whispered, and the cries ceased. Then she turned her face upward, and lifted the baby to show it to someone. A figure stood beside her chair, and bent tenderly over mother and child. It was himself, in his doctor's gown and his mood of happiness—he, Nostradame, with a hand out to Anne's child in the gesture of a father, proud and joyous—

16

Manly Wade Wellman

He started. That had been a dream, not a vision, for he had dozed on the tripod. For an instant he pondered that the ancients had found truth in dreams, too. And then the forked rod was trembling in his hands, and his every fiber grew taut and tense as, in the darkness, a screen of mist made itself.

This time he heard before he saw, a voice muttering a single word, muttering it again. He spoke the word in his turn—"*Atoma* . . . ." Greek, ancient Greek. *Atoma* signifies that which does not divide. But the voice spoke again, adding another word, this time Latin:

"*Atoma divisa* . . . ."

The mist was clearing, and Nostradame shuddered with a prescience of terror, he knew not what. And then it was gone, mist and voice and all, before completion. His mind had been snatched back to his study by the loud staccato of a knock from the front of the house.

Quickly he rose, doffing robe and laying down rod, and walked into his consulting chamber and to the front door.

Pattern of the Future

Anne Poins Genelle was at the door, smiling from her hood.

"I am no soothsayer," said Nostradame. "You are the last person I thought to see."

"Because I am here on your concern. Your second sight is for others—not yourself." He opened the door for her to come in. "I am thought to be in my bed, but a cook in Lady Olande's kitchen is my trusty friend, and I left by the back door. Messire, my head has rung and whirled all this day with the things you told me."

"About days to come?"

"Aye, that. How think you manage? Are you there indeed, in a time unborn?"

They sat, and he frowned over her question.

"More than anything, it is this: I move, by some great power, past a border or fringe. My sight and hearing are not clear. I see as one is said to see dead ghosts!"

"For example," said Anne, pushing back her hood, "did you make one of the company at the joust where the king died—where he will die, twelve years hence? Did none look at you?"

He shook his head. "Indeed, had I been visible, would any have eyes for me, when they saw their sovereign lord so sadly stricken?"

"Then you do not know."

"I cannot know. Those moments are full of wonder and dread. I speak to none, and none speaks to me."

"Sir," she said, "how if you had a comrade in those moments? One you can know and trust?" She was eager and shy in the same mood. But again he shook his head.

"I have not dared tell any, save only you."

"Then take me for your fellow—into the times to come."

It was his turn to be mystified.

"How that, child? I have told you how difficult and strange is the ancient ceremony—"

"Could not two perform it as well as one—better? Think!" Now she was bold, insistent. "It is an exploration more wondrous than any in history—more than Marco Polo, more than John Mandeville, than Christopher Columbus himself. Have you read the poems of Dante?"

"Aye, that. He saw amazements in hell and heaven, were he to be believed. But he was guided by Virgil."

"They were friends together. Two may prosper where one dare only linger on the threshold," she rose. "Come."

She led him to the study, as if it were her study and he was the guest. There Nostradame, converted to the spirit of her wish, rummaged in the closet and found for her another brass tripod stool like his, and a figured robe which he had discarded for its tatters a year before. From a laurel branch in a corner he cut a forked stick and showed her how to hold it.

"Now," he said.

They sat facing each other across the herb-fuming basin. He showed her how to moisten the fringe of the robe. Leaning across, he blew out the taper on the desk. They sat in silent darkness.

"I see light," she whispered, "or is it my fancy—"

"Hush," he bade her, his own eyes fixed on the faint glow that betokened the gathering of the mist.

For once his hands did not tremble, he did not feel the touch of fear. He would have glanced at Anne to see if she, too, faced the adventure with courage, but feared to break the spell. Through the haze came strange noises, a rhythmic clatter of metal and something like a deep, long shout, but also with something of metal in it, like the blast of a great horn. Would this glimpse grant the solution to that two-tongued paradox, *atoma divisa?* . . . The mist was clearing.

He saw a platform, lighted brilliantly but artificially, for it was distantly walled and loftily roofed, a great shed that would house an army. To either side of where he seemed to stand ran a strange metal affair the purpose of which he could not guess—parallel bars of bright iron or steel, in pairs and running into dark arched tunnels at a distance. Each pair of bars was supported upon a series of stout timbers, set crosswise and close together. And foggy figures began to make themselves clear, moving on the platform opposite him, amid a jabber of many voices, shrill and excited and with no joyous note to them.

"Children," said Anne's soft voice beside him. "See to them, herded like cattle. Are they prisoners?"

*

Her voice helped in some way to clarify the scene. They were indeed children, dressed in the outlandish fashion that Nostradame had learned to recognize as of the far future. They huddled and stared with the blank woeful faces of youth in misery. There were adults, too—two gray-clad women with red crosses on their arms and in the fronts of their caps, and some men in brown, who moved and spoke with authority.

To one side, a woman hugged and kissed two of the smallest and urged them into the group. The children were mounting by steps into a series of long structures with glass windows, structures that stood not upon foundations but upon round wheels that fitted their hollowed rims to the parallel bars of metal.

"Prisoners?" echoed Nostradame. "No, their mothers urge them forward. But this is a sad thing. They weep, the poor little ones, and their parents withal."

"Surely the brown-clad men are soldiers. They wear weapons at their belts," said Anne. "It is war, and the children are somehow being taken to safety. Heavens mercy, look to the little girl! She runs, weeping."

A child of six had scampered away along the platform, for the moment overlooked by those in charge. Impulsively Anne moved forward, and Nostradame saw her meet the child, not as a watcher from another time, but as an actor in the

The Timeless Tomorrow

scene itself. Anne caught the little fugitive in her arms, and spoke insistently, soothingly, tenderly. The girl answered her back, and was comforted, and turned back to join the group. The children were herded aboard the wheeled structures, and some of the adults with them. There was another deep horn-blast, a rush of smoke from somewhere, and the laden train moved away on the tracks. Then Nostradame and Anne were sitting in the dark, the vision gone from them.

"Ah," sighed Anne, as Nostradame rekindled the light. "She spoke another language than I, but she trusted me and lost her fear."

"I heard her speech, and I know some words of it," replied Nostradame. "It was English, but not like the English of our time. She called you 'angel'—she thought you a friend come to her from heaven." Thoughtfully he stroked his bearded chin. "A friend from heaven you are, Anne. To that poor youngling, and to me."

Sitting at his desk, he chose a pen. "I must set it down. There will be a woeful war threatening the islands of England, and the children must be sent to the country in those huge cars, lest the destruction of the cities overwhelm them."

Quickly he wrote:

Within the Isles the children are transported,

The most of them despairing and forlorn,

Upon the soil their lives will be supported,

While hope shall flee . . . .

"But I was there with them, among them," said Anne. "I spoke to the child, touched her. You have not told me of doing that."

"Because I have never done it," replied Nostradame, pausing in his rhyme. "I have been frightened."

"As I was not."

"As you were not. Child," and he laid down the pen, "you bring me greatness and open new gates of the world to come. How if we try again, and both walk and speak in that strangeness?"

"Do it," she begged. "Here, at once."

"Child—" began Nostradame again.

"Must you call me that? Not that you mean harm, but have I not proven myself a woman grown?"

"Far more than that," he agreed gravely. "As the little English one named you,

you are an angel proven. But never have I sought the moment of sight twice in a single sitting. You cannot guess the horrors shown me. Wars, the perishing of races, prisoners burned and drowned, rains of fire from heaven—"

"But if we can walk there as well as look there? If we ease an ill, prevent a death, comfort a sorrow?"

"How, in this present time, change a future one?"

"I did it," she reminded him stubbornly. "You saw. The little girl ran, perhaps toward danger. I met her, persuaded her to turn back. A small matter? But next time it may be a great matter. Come with me, Michel de Nostradame. Who can say the future is as unchangeable as was the past? Not I, not you—come!"

He bowed his agreement, and they sought their tripods again. Darkness, silence . . . .

The mist cleared to a scene gorgeous and exotic. The two of them saw, as it were, from the corner of a great open porch of a public hall or palace. Beyond was a square, and beyond that lifted domes and minarets.

"The infidel East?" Anne suggested.

"I think not. Though I never saw Russia, this I know to be their way of architecture. But look! Soldiers—from the west, and come as conquerors."

*

The streets were full of them, hard-faced, ready-looking veterans, with long guns that bore stabbing irons fixed to their muzzles. In disciplined ranks and details they ranged the curbs and cowed the staring, thronging townfolks.

Closer, on the steps of the porch itself, gathered a group of men who by the glitter and decoration of their uniforms were surely the high officers of this stranger army. One of them, burly and arrogant, stood listening to a civilian of the town, probably an official, whose high cheek-bones and deep, brilliant eyes showed him to be of the true Russian blood. They conversed, and Nostradame and Anne caught no words but tones of voices; the official was pleading, the foreign general disdainfully telling him to wait.

"I know these invaders, and what they do here," muttered Nostradame. "Terms must be made with the master of Europe—aye, here he swaggers now."

"I thought they were speaking French," suggested Anne. "This master of Europe of whom you tell is a Frenchman, perhaps?"

The Timeless Tomorrow

"Not he," and Nostradame shook his head. "A foreigner of poor descent, he rises to rule all of Western Europe by might, and now he moves to swallow Russia also. See to him."

A strutting figure approached, neither tall, graceful nor very dignified. He wore a uniform less gaudy than the simplest of the aides who followed at a respectful distance, but he would have dominated the scene had he been in rags. Nor was it his nobility, for he had none; every motion, every feature, bespoke a greed and ruthlessness for power that bristled from him like an aura.

This master of Europe stood commandingly before the Russian official, who bowed timidly and spoke again. Into his speech cut the master's curt replies, sweeping aside suggestions and setting his own terms, with no hint of wishing to hear arguments or appeals. Quickly, unfeelingly, the interview was completed. The pleader moved fearfully away, and the master waved for his lieutenants to follow him. As he entered the building arrogant and assured, he uncovered his head. A lock of hair fell across his brow, dark against the pale skin. His face was set tensely, his eyes gleamed like battle lanterns on a ship's bulwark.

"He is evil," said Anne.

"And all Europe of his day fears him and his plan to rule the world."

"How if we prevent this swaggerer from realizing his dream?"

"Impossible!" exclaimed Nostradame.

Anne glanced at the evening sky, gray and dull. "Surely it is late in the year, with cold weather at hand. And this, you say, is Russia, the land of hard winters. Even if invaders drive back Russian armies, must not they in turn retreat from Russian snows?"

"The master of Europe plans to shelter in this captured town."

"But if it is not left to shelter him? If it be destroyed about him—what, you do not see how? Come, come!"

She moved to and through a great open window that extended from floor to ceiling. Inside was a meeting-chamber, and around a table were crowded the chiefs of invasion, listening while their master harangued them. His shrill commands and statements were emphasized with full-armed gestures and thumpings upon a great map unrolled. The scene was lighted by lamps hung in brackets along the walls, and at one place stood a tall basket full of crumpled and torn paper scraps.

Manly Wade Wellman

"Thus we deprive the invader of his shelter against the cold," said Anne, and put her hand to the nearest lamp. "Into the basket—"

It did not move. It did not even tremble, though she tugged and struggled.

"Am I then only a shadow?" she demanded over her shoulder. "But the little English girl—"

"Wiser are children than their elders, and clearer-sighted," said Nostradame. "We waste our time here."

Time Travelers

They left the hall, and moved down a side-street. One of the townsfolk, a simple-faced fellow with a beard and a loose coat, almost bumped headlong into them—then started aside, staring. His big hands twitched up, crossing himself. Nostradame smiled and signed himself in turn with the cross, whereat the fellow stared the more widely, and all but dropped to his knees. They went past him hurriedly.

"And so we are seen, of simple folk at least," said Anne.

"Simple folk?" repeated Nostradame. "Say rather of those whose wisdom is the greater because they do not muddle it with plans for oppression or deceit. Look ahead of us."

It was dusk by now, and lights gleamed from the windows of wooden houses, shabby and old, along the middle distance of the street.

"We enter a quarter of poor men," said Nostradame. "Here we shall be seen, perhaps heard—"

"And these houses will burn like tinder," finished Anne for him. "Look to the building with the dome and spire. Surely it is a church of the Russian kind, and in the little cottage beyond must dwell the priest."

Some children on a doorstep, too concerned at the coming of the invader to play or chatter, watched the pair as they passed. They were too small to wonder or dread, but they were plainly and honestly curious. Anne and Nostradame gained the cottage by the church.

"His door is open, good man," said Nostradame. "He may be a poor priest, but he is a wise one. We will go in."

The priest sat at a table among stacks of old volumes with the strange Russian

The Timeless Tomorrow

character, and his walls were hung with icons. He was simply robed and his beard was long, thick and gray as iron. Up he started as the two appeared on his threshold.

"Who are you appearances?" he demanded, or seemed to demand in his tongue they did not understand.

Remembering the citizen on the street, Nostradame made the sign of the cross.

"Do you speak French or Latin, good father?" he asked.

"French—a little." The words were slow and accented, but understandable. The priest's eyes were wide, but the fear in them was under control. "Ghosts—I see through you, to the wall beyond. Yet no evil can you do in this holy place. Have the fear of God before your eyes, and return to your graves!"

"Father," said Anne, "indeed we are not dead ghosts, but messengers sent—it is too long to say how—for your help against the ill-come foreigners."

A moment of silence, and the greater preoccupation overrode the lesser. The priest shrugged his shoulders—they were broad, peasant shoulders beneath his gown—and lifted his hands to heaven.

"Nay," he said. "What can be done? They have taken our city for their base of war—"

"How if there be not a city?" broke in Anne. "If it be burnt—"

"I know you are devils, both of you," the priest broke in, "or you would not council the ruin of this holy place, ancient beyond—"

"Reflect, Father," interrupted Nostradame in his turn. "Holy you call your town, but its ways and buildings are fouled by the tyrant. Holding it for his base, he may win over all Russia. Left without it, he must fall back, lest he freeze."

The priest was on his knees, praying. Then he looked up, his eyes wide, but this time joyous.

"It is true!" he cried. "Your words are wise and blessed! Say, are you saints or angels?"

"We are as common folk as your good self," said Nostradame. "But haste to what you must do."

The priest was on his feet again. He strode to the open fire and caught from it a brand that blossomed with tongues of flame. Back to the wall, he stripped from it the icons, and caught up such books as the crook of his big arm could hold. Then he held the fire to the hangings at the window. There was a hungry leap of orange flame. The dry wood of the sill caught. A moment more, and the priest was in the street, waving his torch and shouting in Russian. People ran to listen, and he exhorted them, and they answered him with shouts of wild approval and enthusiasm.

"Hark to them," said Anne to Nostradame. "Are they not Russians, Muscovites? Loving their land before all things—"

"Leave this doorway," urged Nostradame. "The cottage burns, and its blaze spreads to the church."

They gained the street, and looked back to the red glow in the windows of the priest's home.

A patrol of the invader troops was hurrying up the street. Its leader gained the door they had left, but shrank back before a great puff of smoke.

"Already the fire is too great," said Anne. "Ha, hear the tall soldier curse, his fingers were scorched. And see to the Russians—that one in the smock catches a brand from the burning and runs to fire his own house. And others also!"

*

Perhaps the time of the vision hurried for them. It was as though they saw in moments what might normally take hours. The row of houses blazed up in a score of places. Shouting citizens, inspired to grim action, carried torches elsewhere. A great stable was aflame, horses ran from it. From a public square rose a swirl of conflagration like the throat of a volcano.

"Nought can quench it now," said Anne. "It is brighter than day, though the night darkens. My eyes cannot see—"

And the shouting died, the bustling figures faded. Again the two were in Nostradame's study. Anne sagged on her tripod, and Nostradame took her elbow and led her into the lighted front room.

Gravely, softly, they spoke of what they had known together.

"'Twas done," Anne said shakily, again and again. "We, from this our Sixteenth Century, went to another time and place, and did a small thing that grew to a great thing—I tremble!"

She sat on the couch, and recovered enough to smile. "I would be an ill comrade to faint now, when—was I not brave?"

The Timeless Tomorrow

"As the archangels are brave," Nostradame assured her.

"You say you know that false master of Europe, with his strut and his forelock. Let the winter not comfort him unsheltered! How is he named?"

Nostradame gestured the query aside. "A name of no account, by descent or virtue. I do not give it, even by implication or anagram, in my writings. See these quatrains, for other visions of him." And he brought them from his study.

Deep in the heart of Europe's Western land

A child of poorest parents shall be sprung,

Whose tongue shall sway and rule great troops and grand

Until his fame to Earth's last land is sung.

"And here," said Nostradame, offering another, "is my glimpse of his end."

By thunderbolts his flag is driven low,

He shall be struck while shouting in his pride,

His haughty nation yields before the foe,

His deeds shall be avenged when he has died.

"And now we know how he will fall from the point of his highest rise," went on Nostradame. "To think that we—you and I—were the instruments for that fall! I must record it at once."

He sought writing materials, improvising aloud:

"Through Slavic lands a horde moves, dire and great,

But falls the town to which the raider came.

He shall see all the country desolate,

Nor knows he how to stem the burning flame—"

"Do as you will," Anne begged, "leave his name out of your writings, but tell it to me."

"Why not, child, if you are curious? He will be called Napoleon Bonaparte, and when Moscow burns about his ears, the beginning of his end is upon him . . . ."

It was the next night, and Nostradame sat alone in a house that seemed triply lonely and empty because Anne had been there, and was elsewhere now.

She must not, he had told her, endanger her relationship with the proud and dictatorial Lady Olande by slipping away night after night. They would find a way to communicate in days to come, and meanwhile he would scan the future alone. Of that he was stubbornly sure. Anne had almost swooned with the experience. She was not strong enough in body to match her brave spirit.

But, though he would not take her exploring in time again, she had shown him a thing he could do. Here and there he might be revealed to the best men of those coming times, to help them with a word—or revealed, perhaps, to the worst men, and frighten them as a ghost can frighten. And some time he would dare to publish his records, as a warning to the world that would be. Meanwhile, again the strange phrase was groping in his mind . . . "*Atoma divisa . . . .*"

*

A knock at his door. So late—was Anne disdaining his sober council and coming back? He went and opened.

A slender prankling youngster stood there, the very ideal of a great lady's saucy page. He wore doublet and hose of rich purple, with a gay plumed hat set rakishly upon his carefully combed ringlets.

"Young sir?" said Nostradame, concealing his dislike of the interruption.

"I am from the Lady Olande, worthy doctor," said the page. "At her home I am her most trusted retainer, and by me she sends you a message."

"Give it me," and Nostradame held out his big hand, but the page made a graceful gesture of negation.

"Nay, this message is by word of mouth. The Lady Olande bids me say that she was hasty and ill-mannered early yesterday. She cries your mercy for what she sought to do you in harm, and swears that she rejoices it came to nought."

"And what beside?" demanded Nostradame. "For such talk presages the asking of a favor."

"You are wise as well as worthy, messire. The Lady Olande is taken of an illness—surely, she bids me say, it is a punishment for her sins to you. And she begs you put out your hand to heal her."

"Ill, is she?" Nostradame, the doctor, could not refuse such an appeal from his most deadly foe. "What form doth the illness take?"

"Nay, I know not. You must diagnose and prescribe."

"Wait." Nostradame returned to his study, stowing his gear of mystery away. Into a sachel he put phials and parcels of such remedies as might, one or another, be of service. Rejoining the page, he emerged into the street, where two horses were tied. The page held one for him to mount, then vaulted into the saddle of the other. A

The Timeless Tomorrow

moon was coming up, light enough to show them the road to the estate of the Lady Olande de la Fornaye.

The manor house of la Fornaye was a square-built structure of stone, forthright enough in its outer appearance. As they gained its front entry, a dog barked from somewhere, and someone came forward to take the horses. The page opened the heavy door for Nostradame, ushering him into a pleasant hall, its floor carpeted richly and its walls tapestried gaily. There was an open fire against the chill, and a long table on which stood a wine service and a silver bowl of fruits.

From an arched inner doorway came the Lady Olande, dressed as for a ball in a gown of cramoisie, snugly fitted to her torso and bosom but full in the sleeves and the skirt. Jewels gleamed in her hair, at her throat, and on the hand she held out as in welcome.

"Madame, you are better," said Nostradame at once. "I had expected to find you in sorry case."

"True, I am better," she replied, "and now that you are here I am about to be eased forever of my torment."

"What is it?" he asked.

"A grave illness," she said, and her smile was of radiant mockery. "For a whim, perhaps, I made an enemy of you. To have such as you for enemy is such a malaise as one might perish of, sir."

There was a heavy clank behind him. The page had bolted the door. From the arch behind Lady Olande came two armed men.

"Thank you for coming to my request," said the woman. "Here upon mine own lands, I am supreme and peer of all save the King himself. It is my right to dispense the high justice, the middle, and the low. I can kill if so I wish, and at present, Messire Michel de Nostradame, I wish to kill you."

The Most Awful Vision

A day before, Nostradame had defied stoutly the assault of two men-at-arms as formidable as Lady Olande's servitors, but he had been armed. Here, as Lady Olande reminded him, her power was all but absolute, and undoubtedly there were other men within call.

He turned briefly toward the door, but the page stood there with a savage grin, hand on dagger. Nostradame turned to his captor.

"Have you stopped to think," he said, "that I am not a simple nobody of peasant blood? I am known in the town and elsewhere, and my family is as good, perhaps, as yours. I doubt if you can kill me out of hand and not answer for it."

"I will answer, and have spent some hours in readying the answer," replied the lady. "You have been sent for to come and prescribe for me—your servant can testify as much, if he overheard my page speak to you. Well, sir, you have come, and instead of honest medicines you offer incantations and spells from the very floor of hell. We of la Fornaye are honest folk, and none will blame us for punishing you with death. I can and will abide any questioning successfully."

She looked as if she was confident of herself and her servants. Nostradame reflected again on his own misfortune in giving voice to the whisper that had come, only that morning, of this resolute lady's future. How had it gone? No more love for her, no more travel. A death close at hand. He fixed her with his eyes.

"I, who see the future for others, cannot see it for myself," quoth he, "yet I have it in mind that I will see your death, and not you mine."

"How that?" said the page, coming to his elbow. "You're saucy, you man of physic, in your last hour."

Nostradame gazed upon him with a deep, searching air.

"I pity you, springald. Your limbs should have many years of life. Yet—yes, I will say it—you shall die before this proud and cruel mistress of yours, which means you must die very soon indeed. This very night, mayhap."

"Eh, by Saint Denis," growled one of the men-at-arms, "this wizard sets curses upon us all."

"I set no curses, friend," Nostradame told him. "I do not see your death, for instance. You will live long, to repent your part in this foul work, mere dog though you be of Olande de la Fornaye."

"I do not stand and hear insults in my own hall. Bring him to the chamber beyond."

The men-at-arms came to either side of Nostradame, and, unarmed as he was, he suffered them to conduct him through the archway, along a corridor and to an inner chamber. After them swept Lady Olande, and the page, bearing a stand of burning tapers.

The Timeless Tomorrow

It was such a small nook of a room as the rich homes of the period afforded for chance private consultations. There was a settee of heavy dark wood, a small table, and a chair. The page set the lights on the table, where they illuminated an open book. Nostradame, glancing at the exposed pages, drew back and made the sign of the cross.

"That is an evil work and a forbidden," he said. "Spells for the raising of Satan himself—it merits to be burned."

Lady Olande laughed. "Yet you know it and what it is, which argues your own evil knowledge. I myself have never bothered to read in it—reading is to me a vain burden. But it has been in the house, and now it will convict you. The authorities, when they question, will learn how you opened it to read—how I sensed the nearness in the air of imps and goblins, blackest and foulest, and how I, in terror and anger, called my servants to slay you before you did ill with your knowledge of it. Seat him at the table, and bury your swords in his body."

"Sit," the page said to Nostradame, who turned upon him so blazing a stare that the pert youngster gave back.

"Order me no orders, youth," said Nostradame. "Lady Olande, you are determined upon my death. I prefer to die standing."

"So be it," she said, and motioned to the two.

Nostradame had never stood in fear of death. Yet now he sighed over the shortening of life, as one might sigh over the close of a happy banquet, or a gay pageant where one holds a pleasant seat. In moments it would be over, did the Lady Olande have her will. He would not know the form of her false evidence, nor how soon authorities would search his house for what they would find . . . .

Suddenly he drew himself tense. Death he did not fear, no; only dying in vain. Would they destroy his papers, as the vile records of one who worshipped the devil? All his verses of the times to come, the hope he had of warning whole races and nations yet unborn? Could he not protest that, at least fight against it? The man who had spoken in the main hall slid his sword from its sheath.

"This is in a way your own doing, sir," he said, a little diffidently, to Nostradame. "You told me that I would live without hurt after this matter is done."

"Not quite did I say that," demurred Nostradame. "You will live, yes; but you forget that I said you would live to repent, and repentance comes through suffering and sorrow."

*

As he spoke he had sidled, as though timid of the sword-point, toward the nearest wall. There hung a tapestry worth, perhaps, a hundred gold nobles. Now he shot out his arm, and with a quick clutch and pull wrenched the hanging free. He half-wadded the fabric, and received in it the thrust of the sword. A moment later he had come in close, gripped the guard of the weapon, and torn it from the man's grasp. His other fist, big and brawny as a smith's, darted a heavy buffet, and the man-at-arms fell with a heavy sigh, as though struck by a hammer.

Possessing himself of the captured weapon, Nostradame fell upon the remaining armed servitor, who at the second engage knew that he had met his master in fence. He ran out of the room, and after him the Lady Olande flung a curse so foul that the lowest guard-room of a mercenary company could scarce have matched it.

"Run!" she called to the page. "Run, and summon every male retainer! I'll have this devil hewn in pieces." And she faced Nostradame with eyes in which death stood up. "As for you, with your sleights and subtleties, you fear at least this book which I shall make evidence against you. Hear, while I read something to stun your ears."

She was at the table, picking up the volume. "Here is something, in the name of hell's legions, to confound an enemy! In the very language of demons, sir! I read it upon you—*Sator, Arepos, Tenet*—"

"I could not ask a self-conviction neater and more complete," said a sneering voice that Nostradame knew.

In walked a figure in black. It was Hippolyte Gigny, the witch-finder. In the corridor behind him lingered, not a pair of sword-bearing retainers, but half a dozen. The page was struggling among them, and cried out once, then fell bleeding. His death, so lately foretold, had caught up with him.

"As I am the king's servant, I suspected this at the beginning," quoth Gigny. "For a lady to be so glib about witchcraft in charging a neighbor, she herself must be versed in it. When the man she accused stood innocent—well, innocent of wizardry—my suspicion grew. And there came to me now a certain word of what you wrought here, Olande de la Fornaye. I find you at your witch work, book in hand and a black spell upon your lips."

31

The Timeless Tomorrow

She still clutched the book, and glared defiance at Gigny.

"You would dare charge me with that? I am a noblewoman, the peer of any save the king—"

"And I am the king's servant, speaking with his mouth. Take the book, one of you, and handle it gingerly lest hell blast you. It shall be given to the judges. Another of you, place her under arrest." Gigny spoke to Nostradame. "She was vomiting a curse of hell upon you, and I forestalled her. Are we quits now, sir? This service of mine tonight cancels the false charge of mine today?"

"More than quits," said Nostradame.

"Then I give you good-night."

And Nostradame left the raided home of Olande de la Fornaye, for whom waited a grim judgment and a death of agony under the law that suffered not a witch to live.

*

He entered his modest home, and there waited Anne.

"It was you, of course, who saved me again," he said to her.

"Yes. I heard her plan it, as before, and the matter of the false accusation she perfected. When I was too late to tell you, I sought out the witch-finder in his lodging. He went readily to her home." She sighed. "In some way I must think of what I will do hereafter. She was my only kin, and I hers. I have no shelter—"

"If you and she were only kin, then you stand her heir after she is slain by law. Broad lands, wealth, servants." He bowed before her. "My Lady Anne."

"Not yet, not yet," she pleaded. "I cannot go there at once. Suffer me to stay here the night. We are friends—perhaps even—"

"Short hours ago, we were friends and equals. Now you will be of the noblesse, and I am a physician, of small means and simple repute. Lady Anne, my thanks for your kind and saving service twice in a day's space, and I shall live and die your debtor—"

"Oh, have done!" she cried at him, in something of a temper. "You make the gaining of fortune an ill and cold thing. We shall go on as we began—comradely and happy—or I will not touch of Olande de la Fornaye's estate one copper sou."

"Think, child," he bade her. "Think, and then decide. I will leave you to yourself for a space."

Manly Wade Wellman

He bowed, and withdrew to the study beyond.

The driving urge was upon him, and quickly he groped in the dark for his robe and rod. Dampening the fringe, he sat on the tripod. He remembered the vision that had been interrupted, and the words that had come out of the mist. "*Atoma divisa . . . .*" In a moment, he would know what was meant by that strange paradox in two classical languages.

In the front room, Anne stirred with housewifely care the fire on the open hearth. Obediently she thought as Nostradame had bade her, and her thoughts held not one iota of plan for any drawing apart from him. She was going to be rich—well. Noble—well. Influential—well. Those qualities would do for him what he modestly would not do for himself. He and his gifts would be called to the attention of the king. In his time he would be great and honored, and in all other times remembered, until the end of—

Then she started up, for from the study had come a scream of mortal terror, the awful cry of a man who, brave and strong, is undone by a horror too great for his courage to compass.

She ran, throwing open the door. The light streamed through the doorway, and she saw Nostradame, half fallen from his tripod stool, on one knee, an arm lifted across his face as though to hide in its shadow.

"*Atoma divisa*—the atom divided!" he cried brokenly. "I have seen its division, and surely the world is shattered by that dividing!"

She ran to him, and knelt at his side. She, whom lately he had so loftily called a child, put her arms around him as a mother might.

"The riving of the atom," he quavered. "It strikes a city, and the city crumbles to powder—a people is wiped out—surely these horrors shake the walls of heaven itself, and I have seen the last awful hour of the world!"

"Do not look," Anne begged him, and held him close. "Do not look."

His eyes opened and met hers, and it was as if he had wakened from a dream of inferno and saw paradise.